WHAT
GOES
UP

CHRISTINE HEPPERMANN

WHAT
GOES
UP

 Greenwillow Books

An Imprint of HarperCollins*Publishers*

The text of this book is set in Amasis MT
Book design by Sylvie Le Floc'h

Library of Congress Cataloging-in-Publication Data is available.

ISBN 978-0-06-238798-1 (hardback)

20 21 22 23 24 PC/LSCH 10 9 8 7 6 5 4 3 2 1
First Edition

Greenwillow Books

*For the person who carved that tiny
"You can do this" in the study desk at
the Vassar library. Thanks for getting me through.*

SOS

Either way,
it didn't seem like
a momentous decision.

I could go.
I could not go.

It was just a party,
not the *Titanic*.

If it sucked,
it wouldn't kill me.

And, hey, who knows,
it might even be fun.

PART ONE:
UP

8:17 a.m.

Aspen scaber stalk

Blue milky cap

Cloudy clitocybe

Deadly galerina

Notgoingtopukenotgoingtopukenotgoingtopuke

Earthstar

Justbreathejustbreathejustbreathe.

Fairy ring

Gem-studded puffball

It'sokayit'sokayit'sokayit'sokayit'sokay.

Hen of the woods

Not going to puke.
Just breathe.
It's okay.

Relaxation Techniques

Ian spins a Frisbee on his finger.

Kat pictures herself by a river
watching her negative thoughts
float by like leaves.

Esther mentally recaps baking shows—
whose meringue flopped,
whose custard froze.

I list common names of
mushrooms alphabetically.

When I was little, other kids
knew the difference between
Ariel and Elsa,
a backhoe and a bulldozer,
a *Diplodocus* and a *T. rex*.

But I could tell a tree ear
from a ringed tubaria,
a slippery jack
from a slippery jill.

My favorite bedtime story
was the Audubon field guide.
I'd hug Inky Cap, my blue
hippo, while Dad turned the pages,
pointed to photos, asked me to guess.
(He never stumped me.)

Dad made sure I knew the Latin names,
too, but who wants to snuggle up with
Coprinopsis atramentaria?

Wish you were here, Inky.
Wish I wasn't.

Unidentified Species

His Name Is Cooper.

Wait, Connor.

No, Colin.

Definitely Colin.

Maybe Carter?

Colton?

8:19 a.m.

Amber jelly roll

Birch polypore

Comb tooth

Dunce cap . . .

I'm all the way to

Pinwheel Marasmius

before it finally feels safe

to sit up.

Up/Down

On the ceiling,
a poster
of Darth Vader
recruiting for his army.
Your Empire Needs You.

(Sorry, Darth. Not much
of a *Star Wars* fan.)

On the floor,
Cooper/Connor/Carter/Colin/Colton,
rolled toward the wall,
head poking out from the shell
of a green sleeping bag.

On this loft bed,
trapped between them,
me.

Correction

I'm not alone.

Lying beside me
against the rail is
an R2-D2 trash can?

On second thought,
Darth, beam me up
into your *Infinity Falcon* thingy.

I'll come over to the Dork Side.
I swear.

JUST
GET
ME
OUT
OF
HERE.

Zombee

When your dad is the director of
the Hudson Valley Nature Museum,
you learn a lot of crazy shit.

Like there's this parasitic fly,
Apocephalus borealis, that inserts
its eggs into the abdomen of a bee,

and then the bee starts slacking off,
forgetting about nectar, crawling
in woozy circles on the sidewalk.

The introduction of a foreign substance
somehow messes with its system, maybe
the larvae eat its brain?

So many things I can't remember.

I Promised

What Esther wanted
was to stay home,
go to bed early,
not look more hideous
than necessary the next day
in her peach bridesmaid's dress
at her cousin's wedding.

But she could tell I really wanted
to go, that I really wanted
her there. So she said,
okay, she would drive us,
if I promised we'd only stay
at the party an hour,
two at most.

Seventh-Grade Pact

We pulled it from the back
of the cabinet, a dusty bottle
Esther's parents wouldn't miss,
supposedly a red, but to us
it looked black—we were twelve,
what did we know? We thought
the date on the label meant
expiration.

I took the first sip.

Definitely expired.

Still, we passed it back and forth
until the taste didn't matter,
until we couldn't stop giggling.

Outside on Esther's trampoline,
we launched ourselves at the moon.

A midair collision forced us
back down to earth. We hid
the bottle in the neighbor's trash,
pressed ice to the lump
on Esther's forehead,

and made each other promise
never to drink again.

Textual Evidence

Beside a damp circle of drool,
a miracle—my phone.

Time to start swimming backward
through my texts.

From Esther: *Hey where are you?*

From Kat: *They're playing Maroon fucking 5*

From Kat: *My armpit smells like ham*

From Kat: *Esther's turning into a pumpkin*

From Esther: *Jorie??????????*

From Esther: *MEET AT CAR NOW*

From Me: *I have a ride*

From Kat: *Hahaha I bet*

From Kat: *bye ho bye*

Past Tense

At some point
the "have"
changed to
"had,"
and the "ride"
changed to
"did not
go home,"
and the "I"
changed to . . .
Do I really
want to know?

Ghosted

From Me: *Hey*

From Me: *Room spinny*

From Me: *Did you leave?*

From Me: *Ian?*

From Me: *Hello?????????????????*

In the Video

Drunk Me
teeters
on the edge of the couch
like a Jenga tower,
bounces,
totters,
almost falls,
spreads her arms,
shouts,

Kat! Hey, Kat!
Are you ready
to capture this moment
of inspiration?

Drunk Me

L
E
A
P
S

Spoiler Alert

Gravity:

It's legit.

Ian Is Apparently Short For

Inertia,

the property of matter
by which it remains
slumped in its chair,
staring at its phone,

while
Cooper/Conor/Carter/Colton
helps me up, and I limp
out of the frame, laughing,

and Kat says, *Damn, girl,*
you're indestructible!

The video ends.

I watch it again.

Mycorrhizal

What it means is,
the tree and the mushroom
have a mutually beneficial relationship,

that they are separate yet
connected, roots and hyphae
intertwined to help each other

thrive, though new research
shows that when nitrogen is scarce
the mushroom may hide this

vital nutrition from its partner,
while the tree, continuing to share
carbohydrates, starts to shrivel.

It Doesn't Seem So Mutual

for the mushroom to sit there,
pouting, watching Drunk Tree
stumble off with a stranger.

At the bare minimum,
the mushroom should probably
get off its symbiotic ass and ask
Drunk Tree if she's okay.

Isn't that the literal definition
of friends?

Still

I get why Ian's mad.

He was being nice, inviting his ex-girlfriend
out so she can escape her ridiculous home life,
and how does she repay him?

By getting wasted and jumping around
on the furniture like an out-of-control toddler
who thinks she can fly.

By hanging all over . . .

Calvin?

Christopher?

Cormorant?

Crustacean?

Ugh.

Last May

Ian thought nothing had to change,
even though he was moving on to college,
and I was stuck for two more years
in the stagnant swamp of THS.

He'd still be in Poughkeepsie. We could
see each other all the time. *Jorie, it's like
the opposite of a long-distance relationship.*

But I said that all depends on
whether you're measuring in miles
or in all the girls he would meet at Marist.

According to my calculations,
we'd be about as far apart as we could get.

Free BF to Good Home

You don't have to worry,
he told me. *All men aren't*
dogs, Jorie. I'm not
your dad.

It's true, Ian's more of a
puppy. Gangly. Sweet. Never
meaning to do anything

wrong, and when he does,
you can't get mad because
he'll look at you with those big
wounded eyes, and then
you're the monster.

Sure, he can say he wouldn't
cheat, but how does he know?

Besides, it's not like I dumped him
in a bag of rocks and tossed him
off the Mid-Hudson Bridge.

I said we could still be friends.

I Don't Think I Meant to Hurt Him

A few years ago, Ian broke his thumb skiing.
It healed a little crooked.

If it's cold out or if it rains,
it aches. He wanted me to

help him toughen up before
Ultimate season, so he challenged

me to thumb-wrestling matches.
He told me not to go easy

on him, and I didn't, but he
always won, except that one time

I pinned him fast and hard
and felt a small, mean glow
when he winced.

I'm a Fun-gi!

That's tacky, and it's not even
grammatical, Mom argued.
It should say Fungus. *Singular.*

But I had already decided
that the smiling cartoon king bolete—
Dad's favorite species—was
the best T-shirt ever.

For years Mom buried it
in the laundry hamper, but Dad
dug it out and dug it out
until it practically disintegrated,

and then one day last year
I was back at Crazy Dollar, shopping
for Father's Day gifts with Esther,
not expecting to find anything
that awesome again, but, hey,
Shitake Happens.

When We Got to the Party

I didn't want Ian to think I was
clingy, so I dragged Kat and Esther
into the kitchen, where we hung out
in an awkward clump, and I was ready
to admit I wanted to leave, when this girl
Luna—*like the moth,* she said, and I instantly
loved her—came in and started making
these yummy brown drinks called White
Russians, the name of which she said was
racist bullshit, since *the Kahlúa does all
the work, so why should vodka and milk
get all the credit?* and I said we should
rename it, and then Ian came in,
and he was all, *Cool, you met Luna*
and she's like, *You're friends of Ian's
from high school? That's awesome!*
And he's standing right next to her, his
hip-bone lightly touching hers, and I was
thinking this drink should really be called
Pour Me Another.

After the Kahlúa Ran Out

I remember the heat.

I remember the dark.

I remember the music.

I remember the dancing.

I remember leaning back against his chest.

I remember seeing Ian
and not understanding
how he could be all the way
over there and still have
his arms around my waist.

I remember turning my head and kissing
whose lips?

I remember swaying, stumbling, spilling
my vodka and milk.

Random Flashback

My head on
the cool, white pillow.
Someone
is stroking my hair.

So sleepy.
I'll feel better
after a little rest.

POUND
POUND
POUND

FUCKING HURRY UP IN THERE!
I'M ABOUT TO PISS ON THE FLOOR!

Come on, Sleeping Beauty,
let's put you to bed.

Random Flashback Redux

Before we leave
the bathroom,
he hands me R2-D2
and murmurs
those sexy, sexy words
every girl longs to hear:

Just in case
you have to puke
again.

Adaptation

Nature has multiple ways
of avoiding shit. There's

migration (Catch you later!),

hibernation/estivation (Wake me when it's over!),

camouflage (Nothing to see here!),

mimesis (You better believe we are monarchs,
and we taste *bad*!).

Three-toed sloths escape
confrontation by living high
in the rain forest canopy,
out of reach of potential
predators.

If all else fails,
there's always the option
to make like a herd of gazelle
and run.

I Have Sloth Envy

If only I had
algae
growing in
the cracks
of my hair,
turning it
green,
I, too, could
blend in
with my
surroundings
and never
be seen.

Only one
problem:
these sheets
are blue.

Unshedding

Exuviae
is Latin
for
"things
stripped
from the
body,"
and
once
a snake
discards
the layer,
it never
attempts
to slither
back in,
but
hang-
ing
over
the rail,
oh
thank
God,
I see
my
jeans.

GROVELING IN ALL CAPS

The big question before I send:
How many "SO"s?

Add,
subtract,
add,
add,
add.

There.
Now Esther knows that

I AM
SO SO SO SO SO SO SO SO SO SO SO SO SO SO SO SO SO
SO
SORRY!!!

Her Response

No hearts, no kissing faces, no roses,
no cheeseburgers, no pig nose, no pandas, not even a measly
cactus, just two plain lines,

On the train
Text you later,

to tell me
she's not impressed.

Kat in Shining Armor

She's biologically incapable
of achieving consciousness
before noon on weekends,
but I might as well shoot Kat
a text for later:

Heyyyyyyyyyyyyy! Ho Here. Hahaha

(Apparently, alcohol activates
alliteration)

Also,

Help! I'm trapped in a tower!

It's not likely but maybe
the buzzing of her phone
will wake her up, and she can
borrow her brother's car
to come save the damsel
from further distress.

Junk Food

Behind the custodian's shed
at recess, Lance Stahlman

gagged me with his
Dorito-crusted tongue.

When he tried that move
on Kat, she bit his lip

so hard it bled. Lance cried
and ran to the nurse's office,

and for the whole rest of sixth grade,
he trash-talked us, but did we

even care what came out of that
garbage mouth? No.

Ugly Slut and Lesbo Bitch were busy
becoming best friends.

Relationship Philosophy

Kat loves Tinder.
She compares it to going for frozen yogurt.
Why buy a big lump when you can fill up
on sample cups?

a Vassar Lax bro,

a Bard trust-fund anarchist,

a New Paltz man-bun drummer,

a Bryn Mawr psychology major
        home for her sister's bat mitzvah.

Whatever makes her happy,
but I told her I don't need variety.
Once I find a flavor I like, I stick with it.

The Moment of Truth

So . . . that was quite a party.

What time did you leave?

Your friend Luna seems cool

Googling hangover cures!

Looks like I need garlic and a pound of ibuprofen

Let's go to the diner

I'll buy you a tofu scramble

Unless you're too ashamed to be seen with me

Did you know that Darth Vader's helmet looks like a black Amanita?

Didn't mean to embarrass you last night

Really sorry

Not Sure

what

I expected

Ian's answer

to be

but,

it was definitely

not

that.

8:44 a.m.

With morels or chanterelles
or any other highly valued species,
don't plan to come back for them
later. They'll be gone.

Unfortunately,
the same cannot be said for
Ian's text:

You do nothing but complain
about your dad cheating on your mom
and then you go and hook up with
Conor right in front of me. You're such
a hypocrite.

At Least Now I Know One Thing About Last Night for Sure

Definitely Conor.

PART TWO:
DESTROYING ANGEL

Invasive Species

Often the transfer happens
undetected.

Brown tree snakes
left New Guinea
coiled under the hoods
of surplus army jeeps.
They slithered out in Guam
hungry.

Other times it happens
where everyone can see.

Cane toads
were welcomed
to Australia
as the solution
to a beetle infestation.
They soon became
the problem,

the hero that—plot
twist!—turned out
to be a villain.

And sometimes
it's a combination.

The organism
quietly enters the environment,
and by the time anyone
truly understands
what's going on,
the damage is done.

What They Have in Common

Here in the Hudson Valley
we have many invasive species—

emerald ash borers,

zebra mussels,

gypsy moths,

purple loosestrife,

common mugwort,

giant hogweed,

viburnum leaf beetles,

to name a few of the most common.

As far as I can tell,
none of them
show remorse.

Classroom Visit

Elephant. Rhino. Great blue whale.
The standard guesses before
the big reveal.

In fact, the largest living organism
is not a drab hunk of mammal
but a humongous fungus!
A colony of *Armillaria solidipes*
that's been growing for thousands of years
beneath an Oregon forest.

Dad said to think of it like a subway system.
On the surface, mushrooms pop up
like entrances to stations,
but mycelial networks—the
tracks—extend for miles underground.

While the rest of the class
fidgeted, doodled, chattered,
I sat still and straight to show him
that I was proud, that he could count on me.
I was paying attention.

The Nerve

He also said
some researchers believe
mycelium can sense
the vibrations
of our footsteps.

Does it hurt them?
someone asked,
and Dad said that was
an interesting question.

He said he didn't think
fungi could feel pain,
as if it was possible
for him to know.

What's in a Name

Marjorie comes from Mom's mom,
who died of lung cancer a month before I was born

and hated her name—in school, kids called her *Not
Butter*, a.k.a. *Margarine*—so my parents promised to call me
Jorie.

Dad picked Jane for my middle name. He was writing
his dissertation on Jane Goodall's research,

but decided to leave school and take a
"grown-up job" at the museum to support us.

Most wildlife researchers identify their subjects
with numbers, but Goodall gave her chimpanzees names.

Goliath. Flint. Tess. David Greybeard. An adult female
named Passion once ripped an infant chimp away

from its mother, killing it swiftly with a bite through
the forehead. Passion shared the meal with her daughter

Pom. Together the pair murdered and ate at least
two more babies. Jane wondered if Passion and Pom

knew their behavior was wrong, but of course there's
no way to tell for sure who does and does not have

a conscience. Not with chimpanzees. Not with human beings
or any other species of ape.

The Real Reason

By the buffet table
at Ian's graduation party,
I overheard Dad telling
some random uncle
that he *couldn't* write
his dissertation because
I was a toddler at the time,
and going back and forth
to Tanzania for research
would have been
impossible.

So I guess it's not true what
he's always told me about
not finishing his PhD because
he realized he didn't want
to teach.

He must have figured
it was better to lie,
since the real reason
might make me feel bad.

A.k.a.

Mom works as a guidance counselor at Irving High,
but I go to THS, a.k.a. The Hadley School,

a.k.a. The Hippie School, which has a
"self-directed approach to learning"

and "comprehensive evaluations,"
a.k.a. no grades, since, according to their website,

they "strive to foster a pressure-free environment,"
a.k.a. the opposite of Irving, where Mom has had

students weeping in her office over one tiny
minus beside an A. She likes to remind me

how lucky I am that my teachers—of course
we're allowed to call them by their first names—

are there to "facilitate, not constrain," a.k.a. I am free
to be that girl who makes weird mushroom art.

The Hiking Boots

She didn't have the right shoes.
That was usually Mom's excuse.

After we bought her hiking boots
for her birthday, it was that she kept
forgetting to break them in.

Okay, okay, she would admit, she's not
the most outdoorsy person in the universe.

But she didn't mind at all
if we went foraging for mushrooms
without her. And if Dad wanted to invite
the new education coordinator?
Great idea! Show her all the best
trails, help her get to know the area.

She was even welcome to
borrow Mom's boots if they fit.

How to Forage for Morels

They look like alien life-forms,
like stretched-out shrunken brains,
like shriveled troll caps.

But if you've ever tried them fried
with butter, garlic, a little salt,
you understand why they are
the mushroom hunter's biggest prize.

On the first warm day of spring,
you must go deep into the woods.

Deeper.

Concentrate.

Slow down.

Search under ash, aspen, elm, oak.

Scan every inch of ground.

Decide this just isn't your day.

Bring your empty basket back to the car.

Wait, what's that? In that weedy patch
beside the parking lot?

There they are!
They found you.

Record Haul

I still remember
walking into the coffee shop
where Mom was waiting,

how she snapped her laptop shut,
stuck her nose over the bag,
breathed in the earthy perfume
of thirty-four (!) morels,
turned to the Invasive Species,
and said, *You must be good luck.*

Sometimes I Wonder

Exactly how long after that
the affair started, whether it was
years, months, weeks, days,
or maybe it was already going on?

Not like Dad would ever tell me.

Not like I would ever ask.

Signs of Toxicity

Beware of white flesh,
partial veils, parasol shapes,
red stalks and caps.

You can't judge by scent
or taste. (Death caps are
delicious, survivors say.)

Even experts have been
fooled by specimens
they thought were safe.

The first time I met
the Invasive Species,
she showed me
how to feed Tony,

how she pinched
each mealworm between
her pale fingertips.

Volunteering in the Discovery Den at the Museum

Child: *There's nothing in here.*

Parent (squinting at the tank): *Yes, there is. See that lizard?*

Me: *Amphibian. Tony's a tiger salamander.*

Child: *He's boring.*

Me: *Actually, Tony's a very . . .*

Parent: *Honey, come check out these cool moon rocks!*

Me (silently): Meteorites.

Teacher's Pet

When the Invasive Species told me
she planned to donate Tony
to a fourth-grade classroom,
I was like, no way.

He shouldn't have to
perform tricks to stay here.
He's not Shamu.

And she agreed—she loved
him, too—but Albert
the hissing cockroach
had already been ordered,
so . . .

I offered to take Tony home.

He's not exactly a party animal
but he is more active now
that I feed him a varied diet—
crickets, mealworms, earthworms,
and the occasional cockroach
for revenge.

Tony's Portrait

I made his body out of inky cap prints,
added sulfur tuft-print spots.

The I.S. had it framed and hung it
in the Discovery Den as a tribute—suck it,

Albert!—to *Tony's years of faithful service.*
After she quit, I noticed it was gone and figured

she took it with her, wondered if she ever
passed it on the wall of her living room/

bedroom/kitchen and thought about me
and felt at least a twinge of guilt for

all the hurt she caused, but then I found it
on a dusty shelf in the museum storage closet,

just one more piece of junk she must have
been happy to leave behind.

When the Light Changed

I couldn't get over the feeling.
After three years of braces,
a.k.a. tooth jail,
my mouth had been released
for good behavior.

I leaned over and flashed
my freedom in the rearview mirror,
trying on different smiles.

Mom stopped at a red light on Route 9.
That's when I saw what at first seemed
like a happy coincidence.

There's Dad and the Invasive Species
(not what I called her then)!

Mom frowned. *Where?*

Behind us!

I texted him from the orthodontist.
He didn't say they had a school visit.
She looked over her shoulder. *I don't see them.*

Right back there. I turned to
wave. They were gone.

Mom said, *I guess
you made a mistake.*

The light changed,
and we continued forward,
but I know what I saw:

His car. Him. Her.
Together.

Did they deliberately
turn off the road to avoid us?

I could tell Mom didn't want to
talk about it. For the rest
of the ride back to school,
I kept my mouth closed.

Common Sense

I had no way to
prove
Dad was lying
when I asked him
if that was his car,
and he said
no.

Then again,
if he had brought home
a mushroom
with a smooth, greenish cap,
a thick, ringed stalk,
and close, white gills
that he found
growing under oaks
in late September,
I wouldn't have
swallowed that, either.

The First Time

The second time,
at Stop & Shop,
I ducked behind
the avocados.

The third time,
in the library parking lot,
I faked tying my shoe
until he got in his car.

The fourth time,
on the escalator at the mall,
he was going up,
we were going down.

That's the guy? Ian
swiveled around, but
I grabbed his hand
and pulled him along.

The first time
I ever saw Tim
was at my front door,
when he showed up
yelling about

his *whore of a girlfriend*,
Mom's *piece of shit husband*,
and was she aware, and did
she have a clue?

Please Touch

After
the scat hit the fan,
it was hard for me
not to imagine

Dad passing through
the Discovery Den
on his way to
the Invasive Species's office,

passing by all the bones
and pelts and skins and feathers
and rocks and shells and petrified
wood and the sign that says
"Please Touch,"

and thinking, *Sure,*
don't mind if I do.

Eradication

With sustained and dedicated effort,
invasive species can be eradicated
when conditions in the environment
no longer support their presence.

Dad was not in the room
when Mom broke the news to me
that the I.S. had
gotten a different job
teaching middle school science
in Cleveland.

Or, Ian said,
she's just telling you that
so you won't go looking
for the body.

I agreed that Mom
definitely had a motive,
but how to explain
her alleged victim's
recent Instagram pics
of Lake Erie?

Dad hired
a new education coordinator
named
Kevin.

Trick or Treat

Dad could tell
that every
Aren't you precious!
and
What a cutie!
was making me
furious.

Another door,
another stranger's
And what are you?
A honey mushroom?
Well, isn't that sweet.

Finally
I'd had
enough.

I'm Armillaria mellea,
and I'm deadly.

Oh my,
said the man
surrendering
Snickers.

*Don't worry, you're
safe,* Dad chimed in,
but your oak tree?

He made a slashing
motion across his neck
and smiled.

Destroying Angel Poisoning

The cruel part is,
the symptoms don't appear right away.
A victim can finish every bite and feel perfectly
fine. She can do the dishes and go out dancing, the
taste
lingering
in her
mouth.
She can
come home happy,
sleep
well,
wake up
rested,
take a
shower,
make
coffee,
catch
the bus,
sit down
at her desk
in Ohio and start
her day still not
knowing that she's
doomed.

Haunted

My name,
whispered in the doorway,
drags me out of a dream.

I roll toward the wall
to make space.
The mattress creaks.
Our spines collide.
This ghost has cold toes.

I'm sorry, she says, *I just can't
share a bed with that man.*

I reach back and grab
her hand, breathing deeply
in and out
in and out,
pretending that
at least one of us
can sleep.

And in the Morning

I pour Cheerios into a bowl.
Dad irons his pants.
Mom takes one more swig
of tea and reminds me
not to forget my lunch,

as if everything's normal,
as if we don't believe in ghosts.

Nature on Display

Ian tried to imagine
Mom's reaction if the I.S.

had decided to stay
at her job and not move away.

He said, *Talk about a catfight by the*
mountain lion diorama,

and I was like, *Haha, yeah, for real,*
but I bet it would be

more like the bison diorama:
two females grazing

beside the male, ignoring
each other, acting natural.

What if Mom Went on Tinder

What kind of guy
might entice her
to swipe right?

A Chris Pine look-alike,
shirtless, in a kitchen, posing
casually by the dishwasher
to show off his incredibly hot
loading skills?

I guess I'll never know,
since she swiped left
on happiness,
sanity,
self-respect,
and gave Dad
another chance.

They

They were committed to working on their marriage.

They knew that the last few months had been rough on me.

They wanted me to know I could always talk to them.
About anything.

They

They

They

did seem committed

to pretending

like everything can go back to normal

so long as we don't say her name.

Pinched

In kindergarten I had this friend,
Corrine,
who thought she was
the boss of me,
and so did I.

On a sleepover
at my house, Corrine said
we were going to make
a fort,
not with blankets,
but a *real* one
out of plywood she found
in my garage.

She said we didn't need
a hammer or nails,
which neither of us
knew how to use, since
masking tape would do.

It wasn't like me,
but somehow
I spoke up and told her
that wouldn't work,
and she pinched my arm
until it turned red.

Thank God her family moved
to New Jersey, Mom has
said more than once.
She was so mean to you.

But at that sleepover
I was the mean one.

How would Mom like it
if I told her I think
marriage counseling
seems like a huge
waste of time

when it's obvious
she believes everything
will hold together
just because
she wants it to?

Suspicious

Ian sends the disc sailing.
Kat leaps for the catch.

On the sidelines,
I cheer and clap.

On the field,
the whole team swarms.

Ian lifts Kat into a hug,
his hands on her back.

His hands.
On her back.

God, I hate myself
almost more than I hate

the I.S. for turning me into
the kind of girlfriend

who can't just enjoy the win,
who *knows* it makes no sense

to be suspicious.

Scientific Proof

Human beings are more than genes,
my biology teacher, Geoff, reminds us.
He even wrote on the board:

D
N
A

Does
Not
Always

Determine
Natural
Ability!

And yet
he was

Disappointed,
Noticeably,
At

my lackluster performance
on the first biology test

and

Definitely
Not nice
About

my apathetic semester.

I expect more from you, Jorie.

Really?
I think I did enough, Geoff,
by supporting your theory that

Dad, daughter—
Nothing
Alike.

PART THREE:
ART
HISTORY

Clueless

I'm like one of those idiots
who buys a turtle and then decides
it's too much work and releases it
into the wild thinking it will find
a great new home in the pond
and make lots of new turtle friends.

After caring for Ian,
trusting him,
feeding him my secrets,
pulling him close
and then letting him go,
how stupid of me not to realize
he would bite back.

Ash tree bolete

Bleeding mycena

Cinnabar-red chanterelle . . .

First Impression

After school in the art room,
my freshman year,
he came in with Theo,
and Theo asked me about

my spore print and interrupted
my explanation. *Wait, so if I
licked this*—he flicked his tongue—
I'd get high?

I told him no, that it wasn't
a psilocybin, and even if it was . . .

Dude, Theo called toward the sink
where Eddie was rinsing his brushes,
*Remember that time we were shrooming
and you thought your sister's guinea pig
was possessed?*

Let Jorie talk, dickweed.

I didn't think Ian knew my name,
but his smile, the way his hair
flopped into his eyes made me
so glad he did.

Forage Date

It was too early in the season,
but Ian acted impressed
with the winter leftovers
I showed him—faded turkey tails,
blobs of birch polypore.

We passed by the marsh
at Vassar Farm, and the peepers
were going nuts, and he said, *How
do they know that's a mating call?
It's like scientists assume guy frogs
only think about one thing.*

We had a great time
imagining what the peepers
might be saying, like

What's the WiFi password?

or

Check out my new slam poem!

or

*Your body, your choice!
We don't have to reproduce!
We can just cuddle!*

The Female Responds

By the barn, the male spread
his sweatshirt over the wet grass
for the female to sit on.

(The female was impressed.)

I can just see you as a nerdy
little kid, Ian said, plopping down
next to me. *I bet you were adorable.*

Ha. I casually scooted closer.
Six-year-old me would be kicking you
in the nuts right now.

He laughed. *Adorable and fierce.*
My favorite combination.

First-Grade Science Fair

All weekend I worked hard,
cramming my poster board
with charts and facts and illustrations.
The scissors left a purple dent.
My fingers bled Elmer's glue.

Principal Wolbert taped the blue ribbon
to Julia Crespo's dumb volcano.

Later he came over and shook
my hand. *Nice job, young lady.*
Over my head, he smiled at Dad
and winked, and Dad smiled back
and let him have it!

On the Ride Home

Claire, he practically accused her
of not doing the work herself.

Mom sighed. *I thought she should*
label the parts of a mushroom

and be done with it. You're the one
always pushing her to show off.

Dad drove right past the ice cream store
where he had promised we'd celebrate.

Oh, so you think she should hide
her intelligence to make

condescending pricks like that
feel better? What a great lesson!

Showing Ian How It's Done

In my room,
he gently
breaks off
the stem,
sets the cap
gill-side down
on a sheet
of orange paper.

How long do we wait?

Careful
not to bump
the edges,
I cover
the cap with
a mason jar.
*At least
a few hours.
I usually leave it
overnight.*

He smiles.
*Sweet. I get to
come back
tomorrow.*

My First Spore Print

Dad knew it was hard being patient,
so he took me to the park,
pushed me high on the swing,
listened to me whine.

Can we go home and look now?
How about NOW????

Since then, I must have made
hundreds more. Thousands.

Yet I still get excited
every
single
time
the magic works.

Artist's Statement

The color of the spores—
white or cream or rust or pink or purple
or black or red or (in the case of
false parasols) green—can help with
species identification.

That's how most mushroom hunters use them.

I see them as proof of hidden beauty.

Okay, TBH?

Sometimes I feel like
the real reason I make them is
because I'm lazy.

All I have to do is
put the cap down, and the mushroom
paints.

Ian's Slightly Different Explanation

Just hear me out!
Spores are reproductive cells, right?
So when you set the cap down on the paper
and the gills, um, spill their seed
it's like . . . (He mimes
masturbation.)

Stop! You're gross.

Hey, dude, I'm not the one
making mushroom porn.

Spore Print Fail

There's no guarantee.

Normally
I lift the cap
and find
a pattern.

And then
sometimes there's
nothing but
a damp splotch,
a slimy mess
not worth
saving.

All I can do
is toss it out,
try again.

Artistic Evolution

At first I turned them into
the obvious: bicycle wheels,
flowers, suns, gaping monster
mouths. A *Russula*-print
snow family—Mom, Dad, me—
on my third-grade Xmas card.

In my abstract phase,
I gave them emo titles like
"Anxiety Pinwheel" and
"Entrance to Death."

Wayne gave me an A
for the "Rorschach Test" series,
which left space for viewers
to write what they saw.
(Unsurprisingly, lots of
boobs and butts.)

I'd been in kind of a slump,
thinking I was done, all
spore-printed out, when Dad
called me over to his laptop.
Hey, Jorie, take a look at this.

Amanita phalloides, by Chris Drury

A large white spore print on a black background.
Beautifully symmetrical.

Dad traces the gill lines across the screen
with his finger. *They're words. See?*

It's like foraging.
At first I don't see,
and then suddenly I do:
manitaphalloidesamanitaphalloidesamanitaphalloidesamanitaphalloides

Curving out from the center,
row upon row of tiny script.

Wow. I shake my head. *Imagine
how long it must have taken to write all that.*

You could do more than imagine. Dad
leans back in his chair. *You could find out.*

Tell Him

A part of me wanted to

tell him off

tell him who was he to
tell me what I should do?

tell him he ruined our family

tell him I was sick of pretending he didn't

tell him Mom was a masochistic idiot

tell him maybe he could con her into forgiving him

tell him I wasn't that gullible

tell him I wish I had the guts to say these things out loud

but maybe I *could*

tell him in my art, so I

tell him

I'll give it a try.

Birth of the Spore Print Diaries

I showed Wayne *Amanita phalloides*
and said I was contemplating doing something similar.
Would that be copying?

He told me that good artists copy,
but great artists steal. *Maybe Picasso said
that and maybe he didn't, but either way
it's worth remembering.*

Um, so that's a yes?

Wayne continued. *Think of it this way.
Shakespeare wrote sonnets, but that doesn't mean
he owned the format. You'd be borrowing
this guy's template, but the content would be your own.
You could say anything you want.*

First I Had to Teach Myself

to write

really small

Pet Food

In the reptile section, Esther says, *I don't see*
why you want to give your dad your art.

I'm not giving him anything. I hold up
a wide blue bowl. *Think this looks big enough?*

Tony needs a water dish he can lounge in
without his pudgy tail flopping over the edge.

Okay, except you are *giving him something.*
Your psychic energy. Your time. It's, like, not

healthy. Hasn't Esther ever heard of
catharsis? *Hey, go grab me some*

crickets. Pretty please? She shudders but
relents. Comes back with a bag. Holds

it close to her eyes. Shakes her head.
One minute they're hopping around living

their carefree cricket lives. The next minute
they're dinner. So sad.

Maybe Esther's Right

Not *all* art has to be
intense and personal.

I could write anything.
Pick any random word.
Elevator or *detergent* or *snail.*

Hashbrownshashbrownshashbrownshashbrowns

Petunia or *lamppost* or *car.*
Mirror or *face* or *lies* or *broken* or
scream.

Channeling

A mushroom
doesn't need to *think*,
it just stands there, relaxed,
while the spores spill out.

After an hour of chilling
with my notebook,
letting thoughts drift
down onto the page,
I've got eight lines,
all crossed out.

Oh. Right.

Before a mushroom can
stand there, relaxed,
it's got to bust its way out
of the ground.

At the Gym

You really think he's over her? Kat
slides off the bench, reracks the weights.
*I mean, a bank robber doesn't stop
loving money just because he gets caught.*

I shrug. *That's what Mom wants
to believe. You're really gonna make me
do this?* She knows my upper-body strength
is nonexistent. That I'm just here

so she doesn't have to suffer through
the Lifter Kings alone. *The bar is only
forty-five pounds,* she says. *My great-grandma
could lift it. Woman up, buttercup.*

I sigh, lie down, let Kat adjust my grip.
Like a moth to a lightbulb, a Lifter King
swoops in. *Can I give you a tip?* I tell him
we didn't sign up for a trainer.

I'm not a trainer. This one is older,
but they come in all ages, sizes, levels
of swole. *Exactly,* Kat says. *If we want
advice, we'll ask for it.*

Sometimes—rarely—they apologize,
but this one gives the typical scowl. *Relax,
honey. I was just trying to help.*
As he struts off toward the locker rooms,

Kat laughs. *I wish men weren't so predictable.* My arms shake. The bar wobbles. Tilts. The words to a new art piece start forming inside my head.

See, muscle queen. Kat looms above me, grinning. *I knew you could do it! Only fourteen more to go!*

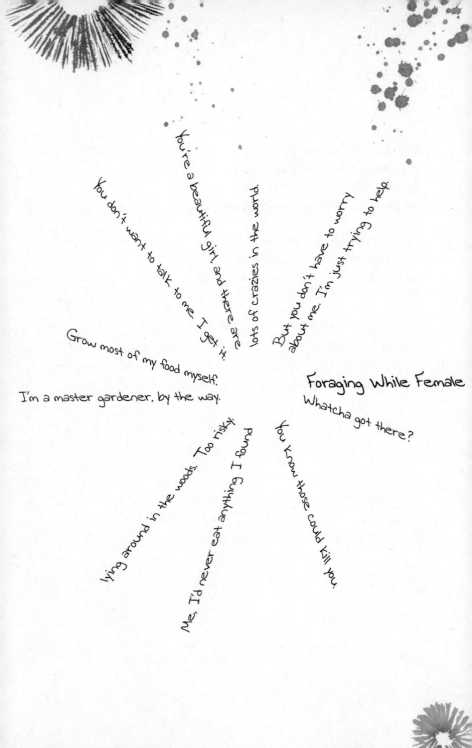

You're a beautiful girl, and there are lots of crazies in the world.

You don't want to talk to me. I get it.

But you don't have to worry about me. I'm just trying to help.

Grow most of my food myself.

I'm a master gardener, by the way.

Foraging While Female

Whatcha got there?

lying around in the woods. Too risky.

Me, I'd never eat anything I found

You know those could kill you.

Wayne Loved It

Though it made him sad for me,
that nature was no escape,
but I assured him it wasn't so bad,

that I've figured out ways to deal.
For instance, I'll bring a canvas bag
instead of a basket, so no one can

see my haul, and if I really want to
repel potential mansplainers,
the bag will be pink and sequined
so they'll assume I'm just out hiking
with my purse.

Carbon Sink

I love Chris Drury's website. That's where I found
"Carbon Sink: What Goes Around, Comes Around,"
a thirty-six-foot vortex of charred logs and coal.

Drury installed the piece in 2011, but it might
as well be today. It sat in front of the University
of Wyoming's art museum. People were into it.
The coal industry? Not so much.

WTF?
WTF, University of Wyoming?
We give you tons of money, and you give us this pile of . . .

Turns out they're not big fans of anything
that calls them out for destroying the planet!

Drury claimed that his goal was
to "inspire conversation,"
so the coal companies said,
Great. We're inspired
to withhold university funding.
Thanks for the chat.

So "Carbon Sink," well,
sank.

Removed because of "water damage"
from a broken irrigation line.

But nobody bought that flimsy excuse.
It started a conversation about
censorship.

Drury did what he set out to do:
he inspired. Sure, they could remove
his sculpture, but not his ideas.

Once art is made,
it's not so easy to unmake it.

Once it's out there for everyone to see,
you can't just pull the plug.

Backstory

Or course Chris Drury didn't have to say
where he got those logs—from trees killed

by pine beetles—or why it mattered—because
pine beetles thrive in global warming.

He could have kept the meaning to himself.
Maybe then "Carbon Sink" would still exist.

Everyone would see it as nothing more
than a cool design, a pleasing shape, an obstacle

to detour around on the way to class. It would still
be swirling across that lawn. Bland. Unobjectionable.

I decide to call my next piece "Safe."

Safe

I start making a list of words:

Mr. Rogers
Nontoxic
Grandma
Marshmallow
Kitten
Vanilla
Padded
Blanket
Toothless

Wayne Liked This One, Too

But

he thinks the title
could be ironic,
since there's always someone
who is allergic to vanilla,
hates kittens,
blames Mr. Rogers
for failing to
make him feel special
enough.

Wayne says it's impossible
to know what will push
somebody's buttons,
so we might as well
lean into the fear.

*Every piece should
scare you a little.
That's the sign
you're doing it right.*

PART FOUR:
NO MATTER WHAT

A.T.B.

It was easy
A.T.B.
(After The Breakup)
to do things together
as friends—

binge-watch David Attenborough
(and *not* make out),

ride bikes on the rail trail
(no water-break PDA!),

go for sushi
(only spicy thing here is the tuna roll!),

sing along with Dorothy
at Movies Under the Walkway
("Somewhere over the rainbow . . . "
oh, all right, maybe just one little
kiss).

The Off-Season

Wayne doesn't believe in breaks.
That's why he always schedules
an art show in early October.
Because if we want to have *art* to *show,*
we can't lie around all summer,
unless we're on our backs
repainting the Sistine Chapel.

He tells us that LeBron James
still trains in the off-season,
and then—for those who speak
MOMA, not NBA—*Georgia O'Keeffe
didn't paint one poppy and call it a day.*

In Common

My new piece is called
"Family Resemblance."

It's inspired by research
that shows mushrooms,
evolutionarily speaking,
are more closely related
to humans than plants.

On the gill lines
I start writing everything
Great-great-great-uncle Fungus
and I have in common:

We are eukaryotes.

We don't contain chlorophyll.

We lack roots, leaves, flowers, and seeds.

We digest our food with enzymes.

We enjoy a heavy rain.

We hang out under trees.

We aren't athletic.

We don't play the ukulele.

We rarely wear makeup.

We don't see the point of microwave popcorn.

We are bad at making memes.

We can't tell the difference between Ryan Gosling and Ryan Reynolds.

Hmmmmmm, clearly
I'm not really feeling it.

Stung

We'd made plans to go hiking
at Vassar Farm but Ian showed up sockless.
His bare ankles were like a mosquito
all-you-can-eat buffet, so, good friend
that I am, I dug down through the layers
in Dad's dresser, searching for the thickest
pair to lend him. When I found
the letter, I knew it was right home from.
At first the words kind of bounced off me.
Then they dug in and I started to burn.

Keep Trying, Bro

If Ian wasn't there
I probably would have
exploded, torn the letter
to shreds, and left the shrapnel
on my parents' bedroom floor.

He told me to *Be the bigger person.*
How would you would feel if your dad
ripped up something of yours?

Not convincing.

Okay, then think about your mom.
She'll come home and be all,
What's this? And what are you
going to tell her? Oh, it's just
your husband's secret love letter.

Exactly! She should know.
Try again?

It doesn't mean they're back together.
She moved to Ohio. He might not
even remember he has it.

Or he's holding on to it
Because he still has feelings for her.
Next!

Maybe. Maybe not.
But why destroy the evidence?

Good point.

I took a picture with my phone
and left the bomb in the drawer,
ticking.

Inspiration

After the hike,
I came home and got
straight to work.

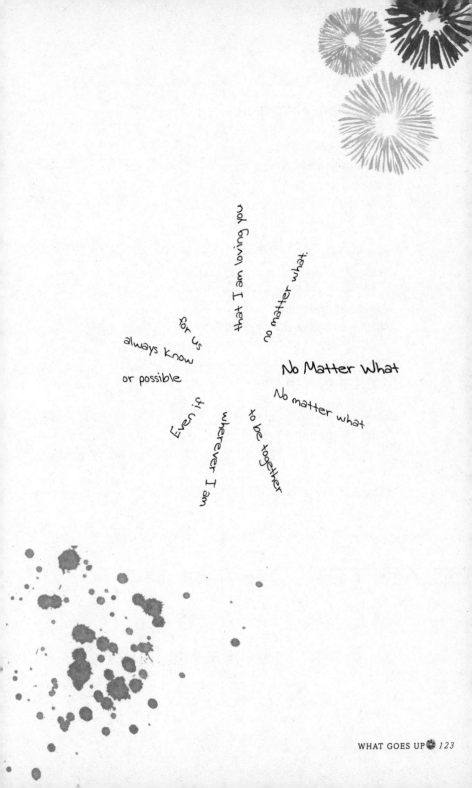

No Matter What

No matter what
to be together
wherever I am
Even if very
or possible
always know
for us
that I am loving you
no matter what.

A Different Perspective

Peach-colored paper
framed with pale-green vines.

That stationery seemed
lovely when all it held

were instructions for
feeding Leo, her cat.

Now it has given me
a glimpse of what she and Dad

were really doing at those
"conferences" while I was

bringing in her mail and scooping
salmon flakes into a bowl.

BTW, I Never Saw Leo

No matter how much I cooed
and called his name.

The I.S. told me not to
take it personally. *He's shy.*

Though now I would say
he's smart.

Better to hide,
listen, watch, wait,
than to trust someone
trying too hard
to seem harmless.

Without the Context

In September,
I show Wayne my work in progress.
He's underwhelmed.

Your text is a little generic.

What else could he think?

He assumes it's my own
bland stanza,
my mushy teen anthem,
that I'm baring my soul
like an emo Instagram poet.

It's not like
I'm going to
reveal my source

yet.

With the Context

Ian laughs. *I mean you might as well have called it*
"Go fuck yourself, Dad."

Rage

I can't remember what Mom said
to set me off, maybe nothing.

A blast of anger hit me all at once,
and I couldn't stop. Calling her

a bitch, a fucking idiot, a stupid—
I can't even write the word,

but somehow it rolled out of me,
like heat from an open oven,

and she just stood there and took it,
so I slapped her face, and it was like

smacking a stone, a wall, a pole,
and I was crying and thinking, *Why*

is she letting me do this, Why isn't she
fighting back? And when the answer

came, I could almost see it, like it was
written in the air: *Because she loves you.*

And then I woke up.

Elegant Stinkhorn (Mutinus elegans)

Long, thin, tapered, red,
coated in olive-green slime,
it has other names: headless
stinkhorn, devil's dipstick, dog's penis.

Commonly found thrusting up
from mulch in parks or yards,
its stench attracts insects, particularly
flies. Hey, they can't help how

they're wired. To them, rotting flesh
smells like rosebuds. Our shit is
their cake. It's not their fault if
we can't understand their perspective.

I wish I could give Mom a break.

Overcompensating

It was just a dream,
but I still feel guilty
enough not to leave
my dirty dishes
in the sink, and to start
the kettle so her tea
is ready when she
comes downstairs
and says, *You made me
breakfast? Am I dying?*
as I serve her toast
with honey and say,
*I just want you to
have a good day,*
and she gives me a hug
and says, *You, too,
sweetie,* and I guess
I must be staring
because she adds,
*What? Do I have
lipstick on my cheek?*
and I lie and say,
A little and rub away
the imaginary mark.

Practice

Yes, our pieces should speak
for themselves, but part of being artists,

Wayne says, is knowing how to articulate
our vision, our motivation, which is why

he won't let us hide by the snack table,
but wants us standing beside our work

at the art show, pretending it's our debut
at some swank Chelsea gallery, answering

every polite question from somebody's
bewildered grandma as if we're talking to

Roberta Smith, top critic for the *New York Times.*
Damn. Kat whistles. *Are you going to tell the truth?*

And Esther says, *Practice on me.* She cocks her head.
Taps her chin. Contemplates the bare wall. *So,*

young lady, what's your piece about? But when
I look at her, all I can see is my mother,

waiting for yet another bullshit explanation.

Laetiporus sulphureus

Fanning out over wounded oak,
this bright orange-and-yellow polypore
is commonly known as
the chicken mushroom
because that's how it tastes.

Not for any other reason.

It's not like it's scared or anything.

I mean, why would it be?

It has no thoughts or emotions,

no looming sense that it might have

made a terrible mistake.

The Night of the Art Show

I didn't have to fake it.
My stomach hurt. For real.

After my parents left without me,
I texted Ian.

He borrowed his roommate's car,
and we drove to the Atlas Diner,

where, in between stealing
my fries, he distracted me with stories

about his Ultimate team, his dorm,
his RA's bearded dragon.

He's a cool guy. You would love him.
("Him," of course, meant the lizard.)

He told me about his classes, that he was
thinking of dropping film studies,

since it meets at nine freaking a.m.
and on the first day they had to go around

and introduce themselves and name a favorite movie
and he couldn't think of anything,

so he just said "*Ferris Bueller's Day Off,*"
since his RA had played it for Eighties Night,

And this girl across from me literally groaned
and, like, rolled her eyes even though the professor
said we weren't supposed to judge anyone's picks,
but I was in a shitty mood anyway from waking up
so goddamn early, so I was all, okay, let's hear what
this chick has to say, and she was all, No disrespect—Can
you believe that?—*but that movie's elitist AF,*
and we shouldn't root for some privileged white guy
who does whatever he wants and gets away with it
because that's, like, what's wrong with America.

I told him I thought she had a point, and he said she
probably did, but whatever, he's still dropping the class
because he needs his sleep.

When We Turned onto My Street

The car was in the driveway.

Want me to come in with you?

That's okay. I mean, really,
what's the worst they can do?

He gave my shoulder an awkward pat.

They Were So Mad . . .

Unbelievable, Jorie.

What the hell were you thinking?

We know you've been upset,

and obviously we're sympathetic.

If you need help, we'll get you in to see Doctor Hahn.

But, no matter what, we're your parents.

We deserve your respect.

Being upset doesn't give you the right
to lie to us.

We don't care how badly you

wanted to see Ian.

. . . *About That?*

After I had spent *months*
building a trap, it's like
the bear shuffled right past it,
grumbling about the weather,
and while it was kind of a relief
not to have to confront
a caged animal,
it was also a major bummer
that the bear was still out there,
and also—also
WTF?
Did they not even read *it?*

Excuses

They claimed the art room was hot and crowded

and they didn't want to stand there blocking the view

of all my adoring fans and, besides, Dad forgot his glasses,

and did I know where Wayne ordered those pork dumplings

(The Jade Dragon?) because they were delicious, and who

painted Elmo as the Mona Lisa (Aaron Kratz), that was Mom's

other favorite besides mine, that one and the sculpture of

llamas doing yoga (Tiffany Yan) and though they were
    disappointed

in my behavior that night, they were also really really proud

of me and as soon as I brought "No Matter What" home they
    promised

they would read every word.

But Why Wait for the Copy

when they can read
the original?

The Next Morning Before School

I go in their room,
shut the door,
dig down through the layers,
probe the corners,
scrape the bottom,
take the whole drawer out,
flip it over on the bed.

Somehow worse than
finding the letter is
not.

Regeneration

Once Ian asked me if I was ever tempted
to chop off Tony's tail and watch it grow
back, and I was, like, seriously?
and he was, like, not even the tip?
And I was, like, I'm not going to
dignify that with an answer,
and he was, like, but that's the kind
of shit scientists do, and I was, like,
first of all, I'm not a scientist, and second
of all, Tony's my pet, not my lab rat,
and third of all, even scientists need
valid reasons to deliberately harm
their test subjects; they don't perform
experiments just because they can.

Regeneration, Part Two

Unlike a tail, a letter isn't living
tissue, with cells that spring
into action to erase the damage.

Once it's gone, it's gone. Like a car
reflected in a rearview mirror,
you might doubt it was ever there,

unless
you have
photographic evidence.

The Solution

When I call Ian later
and tell him what happened,

ask him what he thinks
I should do next,

he says, How about if I
forget it? Because even if

I confronted Dad about
the letter, he'd probably

make some weak-ass excuse
and Mom would believe him,

and anyway, it's not my
fucking responsibility

to force my parents to
own up to their shit,

so why don't I just chill
and come to a party

at his friend's town house
on Friday? It's going to be lit.

PART FIVE:
DOWN

9:06 a.m.

Though it may seem
advantageous
for a sloth to remain
forever clinging to
the safety of her tree,
she can't.

There will always
come a time when
she has no choice
but to climb
d
o
w
n

to
pee.

Sloth vs. Ladder

Squeak

Fragrant clitocybe

Squeeeeeeak

Garlic marasmius

Squeeeeeeeeeeeak

Hedgehog mushroom

Squeeeeeeeeeeeeeeeeeeeeeeeeeeeeeeeeeeak

Inky cap

No need
for a J
because, hey,
it looks like
I made it!

So Long, Conor

This is definitely
"Good-bye,"
not "See you later."

It's been . . .

memorable?

Ha.

But seriously,
you seem like
a decent human being,
and I will always
be grateful you
didn't wake up.

Field Instructions for Navigating
a Post-Party Bathroom

Pick a soothing mental image.
Caribbean sunset. Alpine meadow.

Breathe through mouth.
Look straight ahead. Never down.

Hover.

Operate fixtures with elbows or wrists,
preferably sleeve-covered.

Wash with the hottest water tolerable.
Do not expect soap.

Remember, towels present a biohazard.
Dry hands on pants.

If conditions are truly unendurable,
be prepared to maybe find

a potted plant?
Or hold it.

Bloody Mary

My reflection reminds me
of all those times
Esther and I held hands
and lit a candle,
chanting her name three times—
Bloody Mary
Bloody Mary
Bloody Mary—
to summon her,
and yet she
never appeared.

I acted disappointed,
but was secretly relieved
that the scary thing in the mirror
always turned out to be
my own stupid face.

Two Texts

I'm Googling bus schedules
in the parking lot
when I get two texts,

one from Esther—

I'm sorry too
for not trying harder
to find you last night

one from Kat—

Ho I want details!!!!!!!!!!!!!!!!!!!!!!!!!!!!!!!

Three Responses

It's okay.
Not sure what to do
about Ian. He's really mad

and

Not much to tell!!!!!!!!!!!!!!!
Except Ian hates me

and

they both write back

????????????????

As Much As It Literally Physically Pains Me

I tell them what he said.

They Mean Well

Kat:

Screw him.
Correction: don't.
That ship has sailed.
That's you on deck
waving bye-bye.
That's Ian back on shore
crying his eyes out.
Hooking up with Conor
was genius.
You forced him to put on
his big-boy glasses and see
that you've moved on.

Esther:

Can you blame him?
He's still into you.
You can't just turn him off.
He's not an air conditioner.
What he said is awful
but what you did is awfuller,
maybe? I mean look at it
from Ian's perspective.
Say he broke up with you
and then you had to watch him
ho it up with one of your friends.
How would you feel?

King Bolete vs. Bitter Bolete

The two look a lot alike:
the one you dream of finding,
and the one you always find.

By now you should have learned
not to be too optimistic,
but you can't help believing,

right up until the taste
pollutes your mouth,
that this time will be different.

Easy Answers

Question: *How was the party?*
Answer: *It was ok.*

Question: *What time will you be home?*
Answer: *Don't know*

Question: *Need anything from Rite-Aid?*
Answer: *Toothpaste and shampoo*

See how easy it is
to be honest with Mom
and still not tell her
the truth?

Hard Question

Could you come pick me up?

And then,
(aspen scaber stalk blue milky cap cloudy clitocybe deadly galerina)
the confession:

I'm not at Kat's.

Gazelle Attack

We don't talk
until we get to the diner.

Mom switches off the engine,
takes an audible breath.
Care to tell me what happened?

Oh, you know. The usual party stuff.
Musical chairs. A bouncy castle.
Creepy clowns.

No piñata? She grins. *You*
must have been devastated.

While it's true
the gazelle has strong swift legs
enabling it to run from danger,
it also has extremely sharp horns.

You believe me, right?
Because isn't that your thing?
Believing anything anyone ever tells you?

Jorie. Her eyes shine with unshed tears. *That's not fair.*

You're right. It's not. I start scrolling through
my photos. *And neither is this letter from*
Teresa.

When I Finish the Story

of how Ian and I found the letter
and what I wanted to do with it
and what I finally did
and how I felt before the art show
and how I felt after
when it seemed like all that work
had been a waste
and what I would have done next
if Dad hadn't been a total
slimy chicken mushroom
and thrown the letter out,

she hands back my phone and says,

Except he didn't, sweetheart.
I did.

Breakfast Special

It's not something she's proud of.
But she says she goes through
Dad's drawers *Because I refuse*
to be blindsided again.

I haven't touched
my banana pancakes. *Have you ever*
found anything else?

Nope. She leans over, dips her bacon
in my syrup. *And he assures me that*
I won't.

I snort. *Like you can trust him.*

Maybe I can't. She pauses
while the waiter refills her coffee.
Look, he says he's changed
and, for now, I believe him.

As she's paying the check, I ask,
What if he hurts you again?

Oh, don't worry. She smiles. *He*
will. Hopefully not in the same way, but
it will happen. She rises from the booth.

Holds out her hand. I take it. She pulls me
up. *And I will hurt him. Because what*
can I say? We're human.

The Mycophobe

She's so afraid
of being poisoned
that it causes her
to avoid the woods,
the produce section,
her own backyard
after heavy rain.

Sure, it makes sense
to be careful.
Sure, some species
are bad news.

On the other hand . . .

think of everything
she will miss
by not accepting
the risks and giving
mushrooms
a chance.

10:43 a.m.

Mom says if I ever decide I want to
tell her about last night, she won't judge.

I rest my head against the car window
and say, *Thanks*. Maybe later. Right now

I'm working through an idea for
a new piece, tentatively titled

"Mycophilia 4-Evuh."

Too extreme? Probably. A little.
Oh, well, I'll keep thinking

after I get home,

feed Tony,

text Ian
that I want to talk,

crawl into
my bed,

take a nap.

Mycorrhizal, Revised

By definition,
the relationship is give-and-take.

The tree gives carbon.
The fungus takes it
in exchange for water
and other essentials.

Is there always an equal exchange?

No.

Still, they keep reaching out.
They make the connection.

It's not a perfect arrangement,
but
it's how they survive.

ACKNOWLEDGMENTS

I am grateful to many, and super-extra grateful to the following:

Tina Dubois and Martha Mihalick. You must have thought your patience would literally have to be infinite.

Megan Atwood and Laura Ruby. Your generous tarot readings kept assuring me that everything would be fine, and I think that's what made it true.

Anne Ursu. All those years ago I didn't realize how badly I needed you to pick me to help you with the "Writing the Unreal" workshop at the Highlights Foundation. I will forever be thankful that you did.

Ron Koertge. You may not remember the time you were the only one who called to make sure I hadn't been swept away by a tornado in St. Louis, but I do.

Alysa Wishingrad, Gail Upchurch, and Phoebe North. Keep the conversation and the cans of rosé comin'!

The staff of Crafted Kup in Poughkeepsie, New York. You continue to put up with all the adjectives in my latte order and never kick me out when, clearly, my drink is gone, and I'm just pretending to sip from an empty cup.

Chris Drury. While Googling "spore print art"—a pastime more people should try!—I found your website, www.chrisdrury.co.uk., and got lost in your incredible environmental artwork. Thanks for your vision.

Everyone at Greenwillow, especially design wizard Sylvie Le Floc'h, for whom "Can you make this poem look like a destroying angel?" would never be a ridiculous request, and managing editor Lois Adams, who diligently forages and always finds what I miss.

Sarah J. Coleman. I want to tattoo my body with your cover art. Upper back or forearm—or both?

Claudia and Audrey Hinsdale. Technically, I created you, but it sure feels like the other way around. YOU GO GLENN COCO.

Eric Hinsdale. So many morels! You are magic.

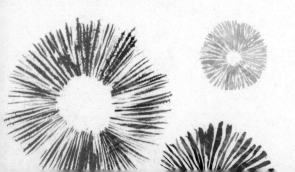